Stubby the Fear~~ful~~less Squid

Barbara Davis-Pyles

Illustrated by Carolyn Conahan

little bigfoot
an imprint of sasquatch books
seattle, wa

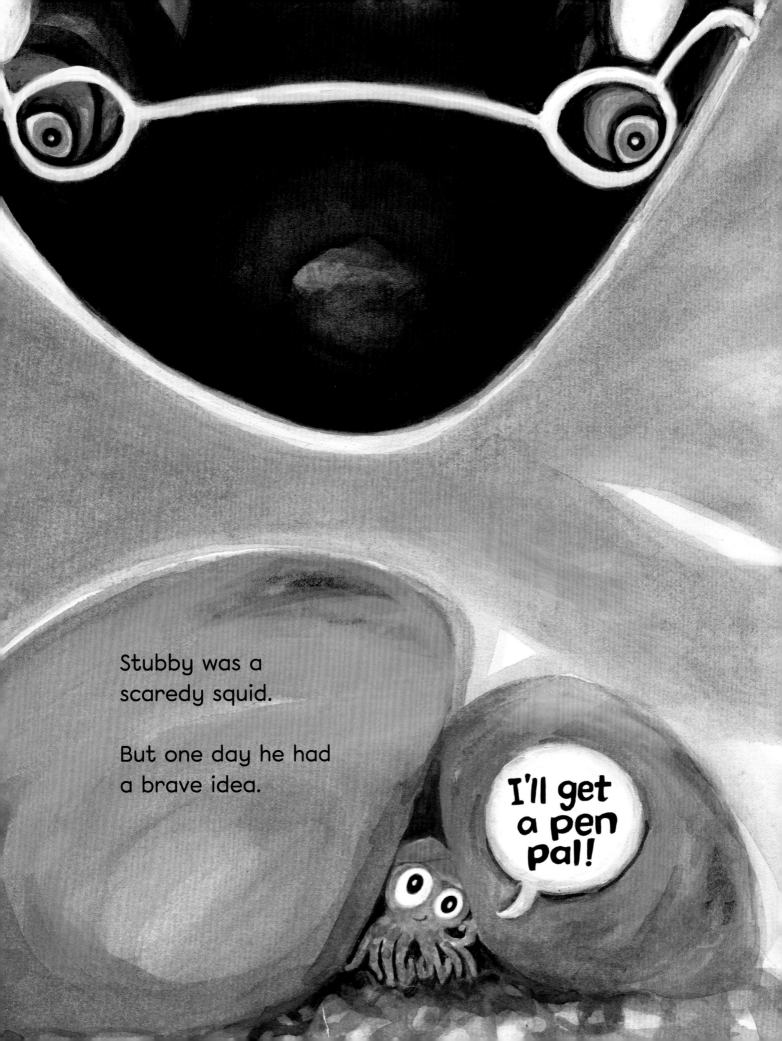

Stubby was a
scaredy squid.

But one day he had
a brave idea.

I'll get
a pen
pal!

That was a mistake.

When Stubby saw his new pen pal's name, he totally inked himself.

Razor Clam.

But Stubby wrote anyway.

Dear Razor,

I'm your new pen pal, so let me tell you a little about myself.

I'm rough and tough and ^NOT afraid of ~~every~~ANYthing! And boy, do I know how to get out of a jam—even when it's a mondo mess of jellyfish! Write soon!

Your fearful~~ful~~LESS friend,

Stubby

Clearly Stubby had gotten carried away and *that* was a mistake.

Because one week later . . .

Dear Stubbs,

We must be fish of a fin! I sure could
have used your help getting out of
a crabby jam just yesterday. I was
double-dogfish dared to trip all six legs
of an Alaskan king, and, of course, he
had a royal fit!

Your daring friend,

Razor

Stubby could barely sleep from all of his crabby nightmares.

But the next day he got carried away all over again.

Dear Razor,

Boy that was a close shave! I had one myself last week when I got caught in an orca's fin pit. Good thing he was ticklish!

Your ~~gutless~~SY friend,

Stubby

Yep, another mistake. Because . . .

Dear Stubbs,

I'll be sure to use your tickle tip when things get rough at the shark park! Last Tuesday, one of the new guys mistook me for a breath mint. It took some serious karate chops to get out of those chompers!

Your finja friend,

Razor

Oh no! My pen pal is a <u>fin</u>ja? Even pirates are afraid of finjas!

But Stubby wrote back,
even though it was
probably a mistake.

Razor,

That sounds like the time a couple of sea lions thought I was a beach ball! Don't believe the rumors—their noses do *not* make a horn sound when squeezed.

Your friend who ~~loathes~~ LOVES adventure,

Stubby

Stubbs,

Do believe the rumors about electric eels! This morning I poked one with a fork just to see. It was a *shocking* experience!

Your bold friend,

Razor

Well, that letter shocked Stubby for sure . . .

because it didn't scare him—it made him giggle!

He wrote back right away.

Razor,

Well I had quite a jolt myself at the Seaweed Stampede Rodeo last weekend. I signed up for bull shark riding and drew Terrible Typhoon! I didn't even last five seconds.

Yee-haw!
Stubby

Wow! Just writing that letter made Stubby feel two times braver!

Maybe this wasn't a mistake!

But then . . .

Stubbs,

Good news! I'm coming for a visit next week! Be sure to plan some fearless fun!

Yahoo!

Razor

It *was* a mistake—jumbo sized!

But when Razor arrived, Stubby put on his bravest face and talked of all the daring things they could do.

And *that* was the biggest mistake of all!

When the ink cleared, Stubby confessed.

I'm sorry, but I'm...not really that brave. Umm... I guess I just like to <u>write</u> about being brave.

And that's when he saw
the otter paw . . .

reaching for Razor!

Stubby was so frightened
he forgot to think—or
even ink!

In one crazy finja move he tickled the otter's armpit, honked its nose, and leaped onto its back for a five-second ride!

When the sand settled, the otter was gone . . .

and in its place was a wide Razor grin.

So instead of having daring adventures together, Stubby and Razor wrote about them. Until one day they had a brave idea.

So they did . . .

with jellyfish . . . king crabs . . .
electric eels . . . and even finjas!

And that was *not* a mistake.

Manufactured in China by C&C Offset Printing Co. Ltd.
Shenzhen, Guangdong Province, in January 2019

Published by Little Bigfoot, an imprint of Sasquatch Books

LITTLE BIGFOOT with colophon is a registered trademark of
Penguin Random House LLC

23 22 21 20 19   9 8 7 6 5 4 3 2 1

Editors: Christy Cox, Ben Clanton
Production editor: Bridget Sweet
Design: Bryce de Flamand

Library of Congress Cataloging-in-Publication Data

Names: Davis-Pyles, Barbara, author. | Conahan, Carolyn, illustrator.
Title: Stubby the fearless squid / Barbara Davis-Pyles ; illustrated by
    Carolyn Conahan.
Description: Seattle, WA : Little Bigfoot, an imprint of Sasquatch Books,
    [2019] | Summary: Stubby, a timid squid, and Razor Clam become pen pals,
    exchanging fanciful tales of their courageous acts, but when they meet,
    Stubby's brave imaginings are put to the test.
Identifiers: LCCN 2018053945 | ISBN 9781632171993 (hardback)
Subjects: | CYAC: Fear--Fiction. | Courage--Fiction. | Pen pals--Fiction. |
    Imagination--Fiction. | Squids--Fiction. | Clams--Fiction. | BISAC:
    JUVENILE FICTION / Animals / Marine Life. | JUVENILE FICTION / Social
    Issues / Emotions & Feelings. | JUVENILE FICTION / Social Issues /
    Friendship.
Classification: LCC PZ7.1.D355 Stu 2019 | DDC [E]--dc23
LC record available at https://lccn.loc.gov/2018053945

ISBN: 978-1-63217-199-3

Sasquatch Books
1904 Third Avenue, Suite 710
Seattle, WA 98101
(206) 467-4300
SasquatchBooks.com

For James, who is brave beyond measure.
– BARBARA DAVIS-PYLES

Dedicated to the splendid and surprising world
full of interesting creatures so fun to investigate
and draw. Thank you, world.

– CAROLYN CONAHAN

BARBARA DAVIS-PYLES is brave enough to write a book called *Grizzly Boy* and have a pen pal named Luke. She thinks skydiving and bungee jumping are ~~terrifying~~IC!

CAROLYN CONAHAN illustrates stories and sometimes writes them too. As staff artist at *Cricket* magazine, she also draws comics and bugs. That's a lot of drawing (and some writing), but she often wishes for eight squid-y arms (plus two tentacles) so she could do even more! In a quiet studio in a peaceful backyard in Portland, Oregon, she makes do with two.